Brother hugo and the Bear

Written by **Katy Beebe**

Illustrated by **S. D. Schindler**

Eerdmans Books for Young Readers

Grand Rapids, Michigan • Cambridge, U.K.

Text © 2014 Katy Beebe
Illustrations © 2014 S. D. Schindler

Published in 2014 by Eerdmans Books for Young Readers,
an imprint of Wm. B. Eerdmans Publishing Co.
2140 Oak Industrial Dr. NE
Grand Rapids, Michigan 49505
P.O. Box 163, Cambridge CB3 9PU U.K.

www.eerdmans.com/youngreaders

Manufactured at Tien Wah Press
in Malaysia in October 2013, first printing

20 19 18 17 16 15 14   9 8 7 6 5 4 3 2 1

Library of Congress Cataloging-in-Publication Data

Beebe, Katy.
Brother Hugo and the bear / by Katy Beebe; illustrated by S.D. Schindler.
pages cm
Loosely based on a note found in a twelfth-century manuscript.
Summary: After painstakingly crafting a new copy of a destroyed library book,
a monk tries to protect it from a hungry bear with a taste for literature. Includes
historical note on medieval illuminated manuscripts.
ISBN 978-0-8028-5407-0
[1. Books and reading – Fiction. 2. Manuscripts – Fiction. 3. Monks – Fiction.
4. Bears – Fiction. 5. Middle Ages – Fiction.] I. Schindler, S. D., illustrator. II.
Title.
PZ7.B3823Br 2014
[E] – dc23
2013031001

The illustrations were rendered in ink and watercolor.
The text type was set in Catull.

The quote from Peter the Venerable in the historical note comes from Letter 24,
"Ad Cartusienses," in Giles Constable (ed.), *The Letters of Peter the Venerable*,
Vol. I (Cambridge, MA: Harvard University Press, 1967), pp. 44-47.

FSC
www.fsc.org
MIX
Paper from
responsible sources
FSC® C012700

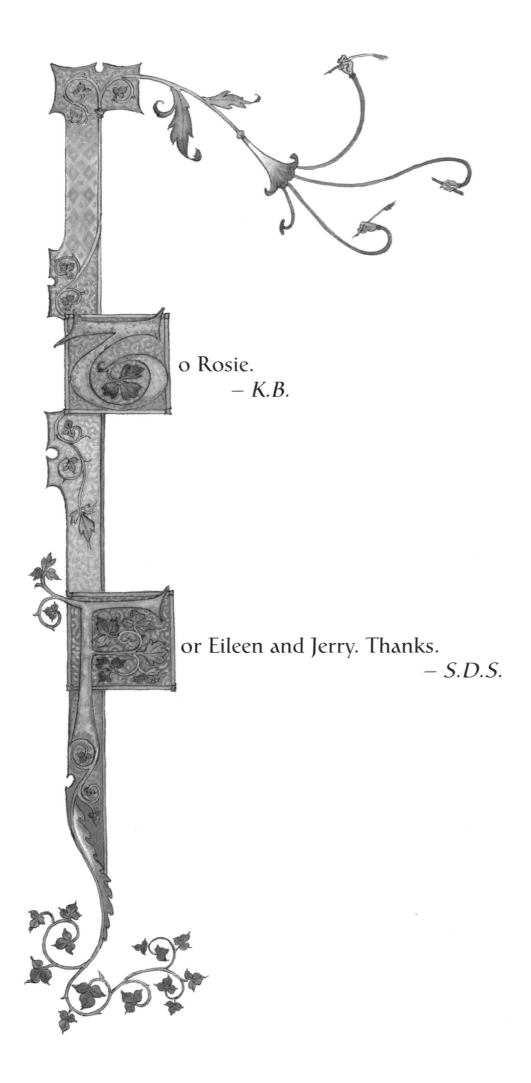

o Rosie.
　　　　　　— *K.B.*

or Eileen and Jerry. Thanks.
　　　　　　　　　　— *S.D.S.*

t befell that on the first day of Lent, Brother Hugo could not return his library book. "I shall have to inform the Abbot of this, Brother Hugo," said the librarian.

he Abbot was most displeased. "Our house now lacks the comforting letters of St. Augustine, Brother Hugo. How did this happen?"

ather Abbot," said Brother Hugo, "truly, the words of St. Augustine are as sweet as honeycomb to me. But I am afraid they were much the sweeter to the bear."

ear, Brother Hugo?"

"Yes, Father."

"Pray tell, Brother Hugo," said the Abbot, "how did a bear find our letters of St. Augustine?"

"They seemed to agree with him."

The Abbot shook his head. "Books in bears' stomachs do monks no good. You must make up for what you have lost. Fetch a copy of St. Augustine from our brothers at the Grande Chartreuse and write it out – word for word and line for line – and then return the book thither.

Do all this within the season of Lent, and you will have made right good penance for the loss. And Brother Hugo," added the Abbot, "do not misplace this copy as well."

So Brother Hugo set forth for the monastery of the Grande Chartreuse. He sorely sighed and sorrowed in his heart, for he knew that once a bear has a taste of letters, his love of books grows much the more.

Verily, as Brother Hugo toiled up the path, he heard a great snuffling in the woods, and so he walked the faster.

Crossing the river, Brother Hugo thought he heard lipsmacking full close behind him. Then it must be said that he walked very quickly indeed.

When Brother Hugo was in sight of the Grande Chartreuse, there came such grumblings and growlings in his ear that he sped full mightily through the fields and orchards and gardens and buildings, and through the gate and across the courtyard and into the cloister, and he did not cease until he found the great Prior of the Grande Chartreuse.

less me!" said the Prior, "How came you to be so eager to visit us, Brother Hugo?"

When Brother Hugo revealed the cause of his haste, the Prior sighed. "Of course you may borrow our copy of St. Augustine's letters. Just remember that books are food for the souls of men, not for the stomachs of bears."

rother Hugo's relief did not last long, however.
He could well hear what waited for him
outside the gates.

et after twenty Hail Marys, Brother Hugo thought to himself that the snuffling sounded very much like snoring. And so by tiptoe and the light of the moon, he crept back unto his own abbey.

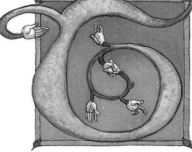

ut all was not well.
The Chartreuse manuscript
felt as large in his hands as a giant stone on
his heart. How was he to make another,
all by himself?

ake comfort," said
Brother Aelred.
"Friends meet every
misfortune joyfully and help to bear
each other's burdens."

And truly, Brother Hugo found
this to be so.

rother Caedmon gave him a fluffy sheepskin.

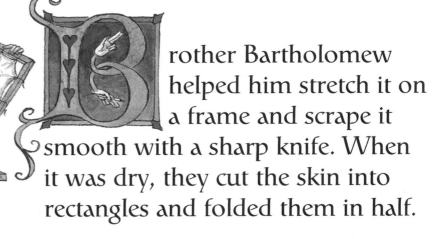rother Bartholomew helped him stretch it on a frame and scrape it smooth with a sharp knife. When it was dry, they cut the skin into rectangles and folded them in half.

rother Hildebert helped him gather the parchment sheets and draw straight lines across them, so his writing would not wander.

Brother Martin gave him a goose feather to use for a pen.

Brother Eadmer crushed up nutgalls, and Brother Hugo soaked them in rainwater for three days.

Now," said Brother Eadmer, "add green vitriol and a dash of gum, and voilà! Ink!"

"Don't forget the red, the blue, and the gold," said Brother Anselm.

Brother Jerome offered him a desk to write at and a penknife to scrape off mistakes.

hereafter, each day during Lent, Brother Hugo sat in the scriptorium writing out the book — letter by letter, line by line. His back ached with many a pain. The light was poor. His fingers froze. Yet all these complaints would have been full easy to endure if it had not been for the snuffling.

"Brother Hugo, Brother Hugo," the other monks cried, "what can be the meaning of that noise? It is like the rumbling of a great stomach or the whooshing of a fierce wind!"

Brother Hugo knew right well the cause, and so he formed the letters all the faster, lest in his delay the bear might grow the hungrier.

ne day Brother Hugo painted the last stroke of the last curlicue of the last picture on the last page of the book.

rother Ralph gave him a needle to sew all the gathered pages in place.

rother Hugo bound it all together between two wooden boards covered in leather, with two clasps to keep it shut. It was finished.

ell done, Brother Hugo," said the Abbot. "The Grande Chartreuse will be most glad to have their book returned unto them."

"Don't forget these," whispered Brother Felix. "We all added something."

hus Brother Hugo set out once more for the monastery of the Grande Chartreuse, this time with a full heavy sack.

s Brother Hugo toiled
up the path, he heard the
snuffling that he right well
expected. Shaking and quaking,
he reached into his sack and
brought forth a poem written by Brother Felix
on a leaf of parchment. He tossed it to the bear
and went quickly down the path.

Yet even as he crossed the river, the bear was no further from him than when he began, but rather the closer.

Brother Hugo pulled out another leaf – a sermon by Brother Ambrose – and threw it behind him. But he heard such smackings and munchings that he sped all the more, dropping poems and sermons and moral tales as he went.

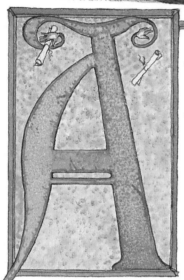

As fast as the monk ran, the bear — who was right glad and pleased with the brothers' work — shambled the faster . . . and Brother Hugo's sack grew lighter all the while. Truly then did he begin to hasten. Faster and faster, monk and bear raced through the Grande Chartreuse's fields and orchards and gardens and buildings, until, at the very doors of the great gate, Brother Hugo stopped.

e pulled the last item out of his sack –
the Grande Chartreuse's copy of
the letters of St. Augustine – and with it,
he smote a great smiting upon the snout of the bear.

But the bear, sniffing the fine parchment and ink, gave a great smile (as bears are wont to do) and gulped down the choice morsel, every bit.

hen, with a full stomach, the bear laid himself at Brother Hugo's feet and slept.

Timidly, the brothers of the Grande Chartreuse approached.

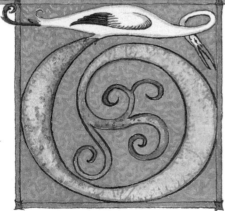

hey marveled at the sight of the
monk and his new friend.

"We are most right glad to see you,
Brother Hugo," they whispered.
"Your library book is due today."

Historical Note

In the Middle Ages, monks like Brother Hugo lived together in large buildings called monasteries so that they could pray, work, and serve God. One way of serving God was to pass on wisdom by making copies of books. It took many long months to make a book because each letter, of each word, of each page, of each book, was written out by hand.

This is why these books are called manuscripts (from *manus*, the Latin word for "hand," and *scriptum*, Latin for "something written"). Because the holy words they wrote in these manuscripts were so important to them, the monks used brightly colored ink and paint and even gold to make the manuscripts as beautiful as possible. The gold in the manuscripts would catch the light as readers turned the pages. We call these works "illuminated manuscripts" today, after the Latin word for giving light to something: *illuminare.*

In the twelfth century, in what is now modern France, two communities of monks were particularly famous for their learning and books: the Benedictine monastery of Cluny, led by the energetic abbot Peter the Venerable, and the Cistercian Priory of La Grande Chartreuse, headed by Prior Guigo (pronounced "GWEE-joe"). They each formed great libraries and wrote to each other often, discussing ideas and exchanging books. Once, Peter asked for a loan. He wanted to replace a manuscript that had been lost by brothers who had gone to a remote location to pray. Apparently, the perils of the soul were not the only dangers there. Peter wrote: "And send to us, if it pleases you, the great volume of letters by the holy father Augustine, which contains his letters to Saint Jerome, and Saint Jerome's to him. For it happens that the greater part of our volume was eaten by a bear."

Truly, with books as beautiful and as interesting as those made by Hugo, Peter, Guigo, and their brothers, who could blame the bear?

 lossary

Abbey – A monastery or community of monks.

Abbot – The head of an abbey or monastery. From the Aramaic word *abba,* meaning "father." See also Prior.

St. Augustine (354 – 430 CE) – A writer, theologian, and bishop, considered to be one of the fathers of the Christian church and revered as a spiritual authority in the Middle Ages.

Cloister – A covered walkway in the center of a monastery. Sometimes also used to mean a monastery in general.

La Grande Chartreuse – A community of monks in what is today southeastern France. Founded in 1084 CE by St. Bruno.

Green vitriol – An old name for the chemical compound ferrous (or iron) sulfate, which was an ingredient in medieval ink.

Gum – Not for chewing! Medieval "gum" was sap that oozed from particular trees and was mixed with nutgall, green vitriol, and water to make ink that would flow easily from the pen but also be sticky enough to stay on the paper.

Hail Mary – A prayer to the Virgin Mary. Its title and first words (in Latin, *Ave Maria*) come from the greeting of the angel Gabriel to Mary.

Lent – A holy season of preparation, prayer, and fasting that takes place during the forty days before Easter.

Nutgall – A round growth on a tree caused by insect larvae. The galls on oak trees were crushed and added to other ingredients to make a rich, dark ink.

Parchment – Part of an animal skin (usually from a cow or sheep) that has been prepared as a surface for writing by stretching and scraping it. Also called vellum.

Penance – An act or set of actions done to make amends for committing a sin. From the Latin *poena,* for "punishment."

Prior – Like an abbot, the head of a community of monks. Different communities used different names to describe their leaders.

Scriptorium – A room in a monastery where monks gathered to write, copy, or illuminate manuscripts.

Author's Note

The scent of books often hangs in the air of the medieval university town of Oxford. If you walk over the cobblestones of Radcliffe Square at just the right time, the aroma of paper, parchment, ink, and glue wafts up from vents in the pavement, hinting at miles of hidden book storage tunnels just underneath the nearby Bodleian Library. For centuries, the men and women of Oxford have been in the business of making books together, and when I was studying there, this tradition of bookmaking and cooperation came together for me in this book. I found inspiration for the figure of Brother Hugo himself in an Oxford manuscript. At the end of an eleventh-century copy of St. Jerome's Commentary on Isaiah, now kept in the Bodleian Library, I came across the endearing self-portrait of a Benedictine monk who had labeled his picture *Hugo pictor*: "the painter Hugo."

As Brother Hugo found joy in the many friends who helped him with his work, my own work on his story was made possible by friends and family. My doctoral supervisor, Lesley Smith, first gave me the kernel of the idea in a lively discussion at Oxford's Medieval Church and Culture seminar, in which she mentioned the difficulties that Peter the Venerable had encountered with a manuscript and a bear. She later pointed me to Peter's letter describing that unfortunate incident and provided expert advice on certain questions of historical accuracy, including manuscript production. Martin Kauffmann and Andrew Honey of the Bodleian Library provided their kind help and knowledge about eleventh-century manuscript bindings. In addition to being an excellent writing coach, Cheryl Klein offered feedback on the very first version of this story, and she helped Brother Hugo find a publishing home. Kathleen Merz gave Brother Hugo that home, as well as the benefit of her sharp-eyed editing skills. My mother, Penny — children's literature expert and storytime lady extraordinaire — provided sound criticism. Over the past several years, Joshua, my husband, comrade, and friend, has cheerfully helped me to refine Brother Hugo's story. Finally, my deepest thanks again must go to Lesley and Martin, who have made so many things possible.

– Katy Beebe

Illustrator's Note

After reading this story and doing some research into medieval illuminators and their methods of work, I realized that I'm a sort of modern-day Brother Hugo. The book you are holding has been put together completely by machines. But the art in this book was originally handmade by me, the illustrator, using a process that in many ways is very similar to Hugo's.

Some of my tools were different than Hugo's, of course: instead of stretched sheepskin, I used watercolor paper, made of plant fibers. Hugo fashioned an ink pen by sharpening the end of a bird's feather to a point; I bought a pen with a tip shaped just like Hugo's pointed feather shaft, but made out of metal and attached to a plastic handle. And while the monastery produced everything Hugo needed to create a decorated manuscript, I bought my materials at an art supply store.

Some things, however, have barely changed since Hugo's time. To apply color washes, both Hugo and I used brushes made out of animal hair attached to a wooden handle. Artists both then and now lay out their pages with straightedges and pencils. Both Hugo and I started by sketching out our drawings for every page. At this stage I showed the drawings to the art director and the editor so they could see my ideas and comment on them. Perhaps Hugo went to one of the more experienced monks for approval at this stage too — maybe even the Father Abbot. And like Brother Hugo, once I began using color and ink, if I made a mistake (which I did a lot), I could erase it by scraping the paper with a sharp blade.

Then and now, the creation of a book begins with the story — the words. The illustrator or illuminator then tries to visually portray what he or she has read. Sometimes the pictures go beyond just telling the story, though. Artists always bring their own viewpoint to illustrations. Often they will introduce new ideas or add decorative elements. Monks like Hugo were very fond of doing this too. They would fill a page with big fancy capital letters and marginal drawings of fantastical creatures and scenes of life as they experienced it — full of color and humor.

Brother Hugo didn't have as much time as he probably would have liked to decorate his manuscript, but if he had, I'm sure he would have included plenty of bears!

— S. D. Schindler